ORCA
YOUNG
READERS

Meeting Miss 405

Lois Peterson

ORCA BOOK PUBLISHERS

Library and Archives Canada Cataloguing in Publication

Peterson, Lois, 1952-
Meeting Miss 405 / written by Lois Peterson.

(Orca young readers)
ISBN 978-1-55469-015-2

I. Title. II. Series.

PS8631.E832M43 2008   jC813'.6   C2008-903016-8

First published in the United States, 2008
Library of Congress Control Number: 2008928547

Summary: Tansy's mother is at a clinic being treated for depression,
her father is busy at work and her new babysitter is
old, wrinkly and meditates while she does calligraphy.

Orca Book Publishers gratefully acknowledges the support for its publishing programs
provided by the following agencies: the Government of Canada through the Book
Publishing Industry Development Program and the Canada Council for the Arts,
and the Province of British Columbia through the
BC Arts Council and the Book Publishing Tax Credit.

Cover artwork by Peter Ferguson
Author photo by Deanna Scott

ORCA BOOK PUBLISHERS
PO Box 5626, STN. B
VICTORIA, BC CANADA
V8R 6S4

ORCA BOOK PUBLISHERS
PO Box 468
CUSTER, WA USA
98240-0468

www.orcabook.com
Printed and bound in Canada.

11 10 09 08 • 4 3 2 1

This is for Doug and Holly.
Always with love.

Acknowledgments

My parents, Jo and Bill Peterson, taught me a love of words and stories. My brother Stephen and sister Judith shared many childhood books with me. My fellow writers (too many to name here—I hope they know who they are) listened to, read and advised me on my work over the years. My writing teachers and students challenged me to learn more. And my first "kid reader," Sophie Vecchiato, and lovely librarian, Linda Neumann, both offered useful comments on Tansy's story early on. Every one has made a difference in my life and my writing. I thank them all.

Contents

CHAPTER 1

Meeting Miss 405

When Dad makes me go down the hallway to get acquainted, I walk very slowly. "I don't need a sitter."

"You have no say in the matter, I'm afraid."

Dad says you can learn what is most important about a person in the first fifteen minutes after you meet them. We know that Mr. 104 has diabetes and likes to barbecue. Mrs. 203 has had seven operations and her pills never work. And Ms. 301 thinks a letter from her boyfriend may have been put in the wrong mailbox.

All I know about Miss 405 is what I see when I go out on our balcony and look two balconies over. Every morning she comes outside to brush her long gray hair. At night I see the spout of her watering can dribbling water onto the tubs of her balcony jungle.

Oh, I almost forgot. Some days on my way home from school I see her on her bicycle with a basket in front. One that is big enough for a small dog. Or a sack of potatoes.

I can guess what is most important to Miss 405 without meeting her. Her hair and her garden. And her bicycle. Bo-o-ring!

If I slump down in the middle of the hall and go all limp, Dad can't make me budge. But I better not do it today. He told me twice already that he has enough on his plate.

As he knocks on the door, I measure with my eyes how far it is from Miss 405's apartment to ours. But I'm not a good runner. And Dad would catch me before I got there. Dad knocks again.

I stare up at the little hole in the middle of the door.

I bet Miss 405 is looking out to see if we are burglars. Or a man with a pizza she didn't order. Or the landlady selling her stinky Avon stuff.

Dad knocks again and gives a little wave at the peep hole.

The door opens. It is too late to get away.

CHAPTER 2

The First Fifteen Minutes

Miss 405 is very old. And she is wearing shiny green shorts! I stare at her tanned wrinkly skin, which goes all the way down her legs in little ripples. Right to her bare feet.

Dad pushes me in ahead of him. "Miss Stella. This is Tansy."

"I thought it might be," she says. "Come in, Mr. Hill."

"Call me Lew. Please," says Dad.

Before she can tell us to just call her Stella, I say, "In case you want to know, my name is Tansy with a T," like I always do. This time I also say, "It was Grandpa's dumb idea to call me after a dumb wildflower." Dad taps me on the shoulder.

Well, it's true!

I never knew knees could be bony and wrinkly at the same time. I don't want to look up. Maybe Miss Stella's face is all pleated like a turkey's neck.

She leads us down her hallway. It is just like ours, but with everything on the wrong side.

All I can see is a roll of crinkly gray hair tied in a knot with a yellow pencil stuck through the middle. And a baggy black shirt that hangs down over her shiny green bum.

"I'm sorry," Dad says. "It looks like we caught you in the middle of supper."

On her dining room table is half an avocado on a blue plate and a brown bowl of popcorn next to a whole pile of magazines and papers.

"I can eat that any time." Miss Stella shoves everything to the other side of the table. "Sit for a while."

Dad takes one chair, and I stand next to him. I rest my elbow on his shoulder. When he tries to shrug me off, I press down harder.

"Now, I did tell you I have little experience with children. But I understand that you are in a spot," says Miss Stella.

"It is short notice, I know," Dad says. "Her mother is…"

I press harder into Dad's soft blue shirt. The pointy part of my elbow fits right in the dip by his neck. If he tells this wrinkly Miss Stella-whoever-she-is about my mother, I will never come back. And I will not say another word to him. Ever.

But he makes a phony little cough. "My wife had to go away for a while. With seven weeks left in the school year, you can see why we need a sitter. Just until the end of term. Tansy can't stay alone yet."

"I could too!"

Dad reaches across and takes hold of my elbow, leading it off his shoulder and down to my side. "I often work long hours," he tells Miss Stella, holding my hand so I can't move it. "Sometimes I don't get home until ten. You must tell me if this will be inconvenient."

Miss Stella picks up the spoon stuck in her avocado. But instead of digging into it, she asks, "Can I offer you some iced tea?"

Her face is as brown and wrinkly as the rest of her. Like those rust-colored cliffs in the Fraser Canyon with ridges where the rain has run through. Her eyes are light light blue. As if the color got washed out. Maybe she stood too long on her balcony in the rain.

"That would be nice," says Dad.

"Tansy?" Miss Stella makes a little puffing noise as she gets up. Just like Grandpa.

"I'm not thirsty."

While Miss Stella is in the kitchen, I ignore Dad's frowny look. I run my fingers through the stack of paper. I love popcorn, but I'm not hungry enough to grab a single kernel.

Miss Stella comes back holding three glasses. Like a waitress, with two in one hand. She puts one on the table in front of me. "Some for you. Just in case."

In case of what? "This is red," I say. Iced tea should be brown. With a slice of lemon squatting on the rim of the glass.

Lemon I could give to Mom if she was here. Dad and I despise citrus.

"It's Roy Bus," she says. "Not tea at all, really. But delicious."

Roy who? I want to ask. But I am not talking to either of them.

Dad takes a sip. Miss Stella takes a sip. I stick one finger in the glass and roll the ice cubes around. I ignore Dad, who I know is watching me.

"Delicious," he says. When he takes another big mouthful, his Adam's apple bobs up and down.

"So, how will we get on, you and I?" asks Miss Stella.

I shrug. *Beats me*, is what I want to say. *This wasn't MY idea.*

When I shrug again, Miss Stella rolls her eyes. Just like my friend Parveen does when one of her brothers does something stupid.

Miss Stella does it so quickly, maybe I imagined it.

CHAPTER 3

Counting Stars

At bedtime, Dad rolls me in my sheet like a mummy. I like it this way since we learned about Egyptians at the museum.

I shut my eyes and take my arms out of the bedroll and lay them down along my body. I try to imagine my spirit moving into the next world.

"All I ask is that you cooperate," says Dad. I ignore him.

"When school ends we can make other arrangements," he says.

I'm not saying anything.

"We will visit your mother in a couple of weeks and figure things out then."

My eyes pop open without my wanting them to. "Will she be better in two weeks?"

Dad picks up one of my hands and flaps it between his two big ones like a piece of pizza dough. "I hope so, Tansy. Meanwhile, you know your grandpa will take care of her."

"I could have stayed at Grandpa's too. I like it there."

"I know you do. And you have been a little trouper. But you need to be here for school."

"It will be over soon."

"Soon enough," he says in a voice that means the end of the conversation. He lets my hand drop back onto the bed. "We will make our summer plans in a week or so. Meanwhile, you have sports day to look forward to." He gets up and picks my Harry Potter book from the shelf beside my bed. "And it will take you the rest of the school year to read this. Better put in some time now."

He bends down and touches my face, then kisses me. His breath smells of Roy Bus tea, which wasn't tea at all. You won't catch me drinking that red stuff.

"I want a butterfly kiss," I tell him. Butterfly kisses are really for little kids. But Dad rests his face against mine and brushes my cheek with his eyelashes.

Then I do it to him.

When he has gone, I stare at the stars on my ceiling and wonder which ones Mom is looking at on the Sunshine Coast.

We took Mom over to Grandpa's on the ferry yesterday. Every night when we're visiting him, we sit down by the dock in gray splintery chairs with our hands resting on the flat armrests. As we count stars, I smell the smoke from Grandpa's cigarette and listen to the water *shush shushing* against the beach.

Last night before we came home, Dad and Grandpa talked baseball and stuff while it got dark and inky out on the water. I listened to Mom crying as we both stared up at the stars shining like glitter in the sky.

I sat with my hand touching Mom's. Suddenly one of her fingers crept onto mine, stroking them over and over and over while she cried.

Dad says her depression makes Mom cry all the time. It is an invisible disease that feels even worse than when my hamster died and I thought I would miss him forever. Depression is more than being sad, Dad says. And it is not catching and is not my fault.

But sometimes I wish she would just get over it. Then I feel really bad.

For now, my grandpa will take care of Mom while Dad and I take care of business at home. Grandpa says that she can sit in the chair on the beach and look at the water and the stars. He says he will give her three square meals a day, and she won't have to lift a finger.

He told us that every night after he has put Mom to bed, he will call to let us know how she's doing. So now I try and stay awake by counting the stars on my ceiling, waiting for the phone to ring.

CHAPTER 4

The Nut-Free Zone

Next morning I ask Dad what Grandpa said when he called.

"Nothing to report," he says. "Remember you need to go straight along to Miss Stella's after school." When he plunks a plate down on the table, the juice in my glass shivers.

"Do I have to?"

"You do. We talked about this, Tansy."

Dad has cut my toast in rectangles. I like it in triangles. I poke my fork into the egg. It looks slimy.

"Just eat it. Please," he says.

"Remember. No nuts in my lunch."

Dad sighs and grabs the bag from the counter and takes out the granola bar. "Shall I give you an extra banana instead?"

"One is too many. I despise bananas. You should know that. You said you'd buy cookies."

"I did. But we discovered they have peanuts. Remember?"

"Okay. Okay. Okay."

If Mom were here she would tell me not to be lippy. And *she* would remember that I don't like bananas anymore.

Dad just sighs and scrubs his face with his hand. "Sorry, Tan. How about tonight we go to the grocery store and buy some more cookies or something? Look, I have to get going. I can drop you off."

While Dad shoves the dirty dishes into the dishwasher without rinsing them, I cut my egg in teeny-tiny pieces and spread it around my plate. I eat one rectangle of toast and slip the other piece in my schoolbag.

It is Devin's fault I only have a bologna sandwich and a blotchy banana in my lunch.

It was very exciting when he was rushed to hospital after he had an allergic reaction. His face got fat and his tongue swelled up, and he made funny noises right in the middle of silent reading.

Mr. Howarth saved his life by jabbing Devin with a special medical thing called an EpiPen that he keeps in his desk. But Devin still had to go to hospital for a checkup.

The next day there were signs all over school. *This is a Nut-Free Zone. Keep Your School Friends Safe.*

No nuts are allowed in the whole school now. Devin spoiled my favorite lunch.

Parveen and I sit on the hard edge of the sandbox while I tell her about having to go to Miss Stella's after school. Cats are the only ones that play here most days. They leave little turds behind, so no one else wants to go near it.

I tell Parveen that Dad and I are going to visit Mom soon on the Sunshine Coast. We will sleep under the glittery stars and rent a big sailboat and go out onto the ocean and then bring Mom home and everything will be okay again.

"Your grandpa should live with you like mine does," she says. "Then someone would be there to take care of you *and* your mother."

"Dad would not let him smoke at our place!"

Grandpa and apartments do not go together. He keeps his bagpipes on the back porch and plays them every night at sunset. Sometime he takes his little red boat out on the water and just sits in it for hours. Not even fishing. He chops wood for the woodpile every day. Even in summer when the woodstove is not lit.

Maybe Mom can help him. It must be hard to cry when you are chopping wood.

"Your dad could have asked my *bebe-ji* to watch you," says Parveen when I tell her about being babysat by Miss Stella with the wrinkly legs and a balcony like a jungle. *Bebe-ji* is what she calls her grandma. Mine both died when I was tiny. And I only have one grandpa. We must have the smallest family in the world.

"My *bebe-ji* might not even notice if you came to my house every day after school," says Parveen. "Some days there's me and my brothers and my cousins. Sometimes all seven of them."

But I already have the key to my apartment building on a shoelace around my neck. And Miss Stella said if I was not at her door by 2:47 precisely, she would come looking for me on her bike.

"Thanks, Parveen. Maybe you can come home with me one day and meet her yourself."

But I bet she won't be allowed to. Her job is to make the *rotis* for supper. Every night! Everyone in her house has a job to do.

Mine used to be taking care of my mom.

Now I am the one who has to be taken care of. By someone I don't even know.

CHAPTER 5

Sardines and Wine Gums

I stand in front of the intercom and press the button that has our apartment number on it. It buzzes. I wait.

When no voice crackles back from the little mouthpiece, I feel sad.

I feel grown up using my own key to get into the building. But I feel sad again when I get upstairs and have to keep going past our apartment.

The little peephole in the middle of the door to 405 is way above my head. So after I knock, I lift up my arm and twiddle my fingers in front of it.

"Do come in," says Miss Stella. I take just enough steps inside so she can close the door behind me. "You made good time. I've been busy, as you can see."

She points at a coat rack that wasn't there last time. It has yellow and white butterflies all over it, like something a baby would have in its nursery. I am about to tell her that I will not put my stuff on *that*, when I almost hear Dad saying in my ear, "You cannot blame a person for trying." Well, I can!

I hang my backpack by its little loop on one of the knobs. Then I sling my jacket across the top. I expect Miss Stella to tell me to hang it up properly. Or to do it herself. But she only says, "Shall we go through?"

When she puts a skinny hand on my shoulder, I duck under it and walk into the dining room ahead of her.

The stack of papers is still on the table. And the blue plate. But no avocado.

Now two small bottles labeled *India Ink* are standing next to a row of wooden sticks lined up on a black leather cloth.

I pick one stick up. It has a flat metal thing at one end of a long wooden handle. "That is a calligraphy pen. The shiny part—the nib—goes in the ink," Miss Stella says. "You might like to try it."

"What is it for?" I put the pen back exactly where I found it.

"Lettering."

"I can do that on the computer."

"I see." Miss Stella rolls up the cloth, just the way Dad rolls me up like a mummy at night. "How about a snack?"

"What have you got?"

"The only way to find out is to come and have a look." Maybe she is a little deaf, like Grandpa, and cannot hear my rudeness.

Her kitchen is long and thin like ours. The walls are a pretty blue, and a long straw mat covers the floor.

"I suggest you start down that end and work your way up this end to the fridge," Miss Stella says. She waves her arm in a big line along the room.

"What?"

"Have a look. I have no idea what children eat. This side is just plates and stuff." She pats the cabinet behind her. "We can come to that later. You root around in those cupboards—Lord knows what you might find there—while I tidy up in the other room." She goes out and then turns right around again. "And check the freezer too. I believe there may be sherbet."

Dad says not to be nosy. But she said I could.

I open all the cupboards I can reach and go through them one by one. They are so tidy! Our kitchen cupboards are full of packages with elastic bands holding them closed. Boxes dribbling cereal on the shelf. Everything mixed up. In Miss Stella's cupboards I find:

Three boxes of brown spaghetti. Ugh.

One can of artichoke hearts. I don't like the look of those.

A jar of forest berry jam with a pink-and-white checkered lid. I like the jar but not the jam. I like grape jelly.

Two boxes of grown-up cereal. The kind that the commercials say are good for you.

A box of brown sugar cubes. I crunch one quick before Miss Stella comes back. It tastes just like regular brown sugar to me.

Sardines. Dad says I must be the only kid in the world who likes sardines. I put one can on the counter.

Four cans of beans. Three of the red kind Dad uses in chili. And one can of the white knobby ones that Mom uses when she makes it. Dad and I despise them, but we eat her chili anyway. To be polite.

Two kinds of crackers. But no little ones for crumbling into soup.

A bag of wine gums. I put them with the sardines. I like them almost as much as licorice.

A bag of Werther's in their little gold wrappers. Grandpa cracks them when he eats them. When Dad reminds him that you should suck hard candy, Grandpa says as they are not his own teeth, why should he care?

A cloth bag of rice. Ours comes in see-through plastic.

Shriveled apricots. All wrinkly, just like Miss Stella's skin.

Raisins and almonds and sunflower seeds and cashews. Devin better stay away from here!

Tea. There's flowery chamomile. And mint. One box says *Rooibos.* It must be that red stuff that isn't really tea at all.

I am still working on the cupboards when Miss Stella sticks her head around the door. "Find anything you like?" She sees the sardines and wine gums on the counter. "That's a start. How about a big glass of milk and a banana to go with that?"

I shudder. No more bananas! "Do you have any peanut butter?"

Miss Stella opens the fridge. "Almond or pumpkin seed. No peanut, I'm afraid."

I shrug.

She shrugs back. Then she rolls her eyes at me.

I try not to smile. But she smiles first, so I have to. Just to be polite.

CHAPTER 6

Calligraphy Lessons

I choose a plate with a gold line all the way around. I pick eight wine gums, four red and four green, to go with the silvery sardines.

Miss Stella pours me a glass of milk and puts crackers on my plate. "Can I watch TV?" I ask.

"I have one in a cupboard somewhere. But it's not connected, I'm afraid."

No TV! She must be the worst sitter in all of Surrey and British Columbia and Canada and the world and the universe. I shove my plate away and look at it from low down with my chin near the table. I squint my eyes at it.

This is the dumbest snack I've ever had.

If Mom wasn't on the Sunshine Coast looking at the water and helping Grandpa fill his woodshed, she could be home watching TV with me. We would share a plate of peanut butter sandwiches with grape jelly creeping onto the crusts. Cut in triangles.

Mom always eats one quarter. I have the other three. (But I never get wine gums for snack!)

Miss Stella sits across the table from me. She unfurls the pen holder and starts wiping the shiny nib bits with a white cloth that has black smudges all over it. She cleans them one at a time. Very slowly. Then she puts each one back in its little slot before she does the next.

There are ten of them. Maybe twelve.

I reach out my hand and pull my plate back. I re-arrange the candy all around the sardines in a circle. I munch a cracker.

Miss Stella cleans another pen.

"Where do you keep your computer?" I ask.

She puts the pen down and lays the cloth on top of it. It drapes over like a little blanket on a skinny body. "I don't have one of them, either."

No TV! And no computer! I know she only has her bicycle, and no car. She must be *very* poor. "What *do* you have?"

"I have a list here of everything we might do together while I am watching you."

"When Mom was sick I stayed home every day by myself and took care of her."

"I'm glad you could do that for her."

"She is depressed."

"Your father told me that. It must be hard for you all."

"I don't care." I stab my fork into the sardine and hold it up. It has no head or tail. Sardines are all middles. As I put it in my mouth, I watch Miss Stella pick up her cloth and start wiping another pen.

Sardines and wine gums do not go together. But I eat them all, and I drink the milk. Then I sit still for a bit until the sick feeling goes.

When I tell Dad what I had for a snack, he will not let Miss Stella babysit me anymore.

"Shall we look at my list?" she asks.

"I can hardly ever read grown-up writing. Grown-up writing is a mess." I feel myself getting ruder. I don't know if I can stop.

Miss Stella pushes a paper across the table to me. "Give it a try."

Her list says:

Homework. I already did all my homework at school.

Reading. I'm one of the top readers in my class. I don't have to have it written on a stupid list. And I bet she has no good books.

Old photographs. I'm not old enough to have old photographs. And I don't want to look at pictures of all her dead relatives like I do with Grandpa on rainy days. He forgets all the names of people in the pictures and makes them up, as if he is inventing a whole new family.

Singing. I am a good singer. But here?

Sewing. Mom has a sewing machine she won't let me use yet. But I don't see one here.

Drawers and cupboards. What about them?

A walk. Where to?

I am not about to tell her that I like lists too. But I am about to say that I can think of a gazillion better things to do than what's on this stupid list. Then I suddenly realize I can read every word. "You said you don't have a computer!"

"So I did."

"But how did you get this lettering?" I look at the list again. "If I could write like you, I would get extra points for handwriting for sure. Mr. Howarth is very strict about it. And keeping your notebook tidy. And doing fractions and stuff in straight lines."

"In my day we called that penmanship. This is calligraphy. Which is why I have these." Miss Stella holds up a pen. The nib winks at me in the sun coming through the window. "I could teach you," she says.

"Add it to the list." I push the list back to her. "I want to see you write like that."

Miss Stella wipes the pen with the cloth again. She takes a lid off one of the bottles of ink and dips the pen deep down into it. Then she pulls the list toward her and writes very slowly, *Calligraphy lessons for Tansy.*

Then she gets more ink on the pen and draws a little flourish under the list.

Like this.

CHAPTER 7

Loony Bins and Funny Farms

Next morning Dad makes me an egg again. And toast in rectangles. I poke at the egg and try to get the slimy parts away from the yellow, but it just sticks to my fork.

"Don't play with your food," says Dad. He leans against the counter, cradling his coffee mug in his hands. "How was your evening?"

I was asleep on Miss Stella's couch when he came home. I woke up but did not let on. So he rolled me ever so gently onto his shoulder and carried me down the hall.

"It was okay."

"Just okay?"

"It was okay." I decide not to tell him about the sick-making snack. "Are you going to be late today?"

"No. We finish striking the set today. I have just a couple of short runs to do, so I can be here by the time you get home from school."

Dad's a limo driver. He works for the movies and drives all kinds of famous people around. He says that his job is just a lot of waiting around. Then more waiting around. It sounds very boring to me.

He collects autographs in a little book with a blue leather cover that Mom gave me for my birthday. I can never read the writing. But Dad tells me who they are and reminds me that this is for later, when I am grown up.

"Will you pick me up?" I ask.

"The limo goes back today, Tan. Want me to come by in my truck?"

"Nah."

Dad cleans the counter with the smelly old rag, even though dishes and stuff from yesterday are still there. I smush my egg up and put it to bed under a blanket of toast.

"Did you pick up cookies for school?" I ask.

"Darn. This weekend. I promise."

"Can we get wine gums?"

"Payday is candy day. But why wine gums suddenly?"

"I had them at Miss Stella's."

"So things went okay, then?" He pulls a bag from the drawer and shoves my sandwich in. Without wrapping it in plastic first like Mom does.

"Dad? Is it rude to be nosy?"

"Yeess…" He doesn't sound sure.

"Miss Stella made a list of what we could do when I go to her place. She says I can spend one afternoon each week poking around her house. In her drawers and cupboards even! One room for each week that I'm going to be there."

"That *is* a little strange. Has she lost something?"

"She says that curiosity would not have killed the cat if it had the run of the house. What does that mean?"

Dad edges me out of the chair with one hand and moves me to the door without clearing the table first. I grab my lunch bag and coat on the way.

"Perhaps you were being nosy, and she saw you," says Dad. "Maybe she thought it would be better to invite you to have a look than have you sneaking around behind her back. We had that talk about being well behaved. Remember?"

"Did you turn on the dishwasher?" I ask as we walk down the stairs and into the parking lot.

"Darn." Dad unlocks the door of the long white limousine and I climb in.

Dad looks at me as he slides into his seat. He sticks the key in the hole but doesn't start the engine. Instead he laughs and leans over to rub my cheek. "Let's not tell your mother about my lousy housekeeping."

We grin at each other and sing along with the radio all the way to school.

When we get there, I jump out of the limo and watch Dad drive away. Then I realize that I forgot to ask him what Grandpa said when he called last night.

I hope Mom does not come home today. That kitchen is a mess. She would have a fit.

Devin Roberts and Ryan Lurie are blocking the door of my classroom and won't let me pass.

Now that Devin has gotten over his allergic reaction, he's as rotten as ever. "Hey, Tansy," he says. "You know all nuts are forbidden in school, hey? That means you, you know." He laughs. "Your mom is in the loony bin. The nuthouse!"

That was ages ago, I want to say. Anyway, how does he know? She was only in the hospital for a few days, and I didn't tell anyone. Maybe Parveen did.

He stands so close to me that I can smell his breath when he shouts. "Your mom better not come anywhere near me. Fruitcakes have nuts in them, you know!"

I push past him and walk over to his group's art table. I shove my fist right into the middle of his papiermâché dinosaur when no one is looking.

At least, I hope it's his.

"Is your mom a blithering idiot?" Ryan yells. He has a skin disease that makes his face look sunburned all year round. I want to tell him he should use more sunblock. Then I remember that Dad says we should not make fun of the afflicted. Ryan is afflicted, for sure. Just like his dumb buddy.

As I go to my seat, Mr. Howarth bustles into the room. "Chop chop," he says. "No dillydallying. Ryan.

Sit down, please. Devin. Hand out the readers. Tansy, I want to see you at recess."

I slide into my seat next to Parveen. "What did you do?" she asks. She is always afraid of doing something wrong.

Even if someone else gets into trouble, she gets upset.

"Nothing." Maybe she did tell Devin.

"Why does he want to see you, then?"

"That's my problem," I tell her. When I see her eyes get teary, I feel bad and lean over to her desk. "I'll tell you everything. Like always. But you must promise not to tell anyone else."

Now she nods and looks happier. When Parveen bends over to pull out her books, I watch her long shiny braid swing down her back like a thick rope. I used to have long hair, but Mom said I made too much fuss getting the knots out.

I wonder how Miss Stella brushes her long gray hair without her eyes getting all teared up.

When I looked over to her balcony this morning, all I could see were jungly plants and flowers filling in the gaps between the railings.

I think about Parveen's hair and Miss Stella's hair and her balcony garden for so long that I almost forget to be worried about why Mr. Howarth wants to see me.

But once I remember to worry, I can't stop.

Reading and Comprehension lasts a very long time when you're worried.

CHAPTER 8

The Trusted Other

On my way home I decide not to ring my buzzer. But when I get there, my finger reaches out all on its own.

Dad answers.

I have been so busy thinking about what Mr. Howarth talked to me about, I forgot that Dad said he'd be home! My backpack bumps against my leg as I run up the stairs. But he is not waiting for me like Mom would be. Even on her bad days, when she spent all day at the dining room table in her nightie, she would be waiting at the door.

"Dad?" I walk into the kitchen. Breakfast is still all over the place.

"Here."

I find him in the bedroom dumping clothes into the plastic laundry basket. "Gotta get this stuff in. Want to come down with me?"

The laundry room makes a funny echo. Sometimes I hear dripping but never see any water. I bet a black widow spider is hiding in there somewhere.

I pick up the sock peeking out from under his bed and drop it on top of the basket. Mom's blue nightie and green cargo pants are flopping over the edge. "Remember not to put Mom's cottons in the dryer."

"Tansy. I can't do everything right, so I'm not going to try. I want to get this stuff in the wash or there will be no clean socks or underwear tomorrow."

I giggle when I think of going to school half naked. But I stop when I think about Mom. *She* would never let me run out of underwear. Why can't Dad at least *try* to do everything right.

"So. How was your day?" he asks.

"Dad? Do you have a Trusted Other?"

He shifts the basket to his hip and looks at me. "A what?"

"Mr. Howarth said that he knows I must be having a hard time with Mom away. He told me that sometimes a Trusted Other helps us in difficult times. But what does it mean?"

Dad drops the basket onto the bed and sits down next to it. He pulls me in front of him so I am standing with his knees pressing into my legs. "Perhaps he thinks you might need someone to talk to if you get sad. Or confused. Or lonely while Mom's away."

I make a little braid of the hair by his forehead. If Mom was here she would say it needs cutting. "But I've got you."

"You do. Of course you do, *ma petite saucisson.*"

That means "my little sausage" in French. Mom calls me that all the time.

Dad unravels his silly braid and brushes his hair back with his fingers. "Sometimes we need someone else to talk to," he says. "Someone who is not too close to us. Did Mr. Howarth have any suggestions?"

"He said I could go to the counselor's office. He said that's what Ms. Carlton is for, and that she's a good listener."

"That might be a good idea."

"Dad?"

"Yes, Tansy?"

"*You* tell me everything, don't you?" He does not say anything for a long while. Then he gets up from the bed and turns around as if he has forgotten where he is or what he was doing. When I touch his arm, he looks at me and sighs. "Yes. Of course I do."

While I wait for him to come back from the laundry room, I make a peanut butter and grape jelly sandwich. I cut it in quarters and put two quarters on one plate for me. And two on another one for Dad.

Kraft Dinner used to be my favorite supper. But maybe I've grown out of it. I push the boring orange macaroni around my plate and squish my peas one at a time. Then I lick them off my fork. "Are you allergic to anything, Dad?"

He is reading at the table. We are only supposed to do that on Sunday mornings. "Dad?"

He moves his head up, but his eyes are still stuck on the pages. "What?"

"Are you allergic to something? Devin could die if he eats peanuts."

"Mmm."

"Well?"

He closes his book and pushes it aside. "The story is that once, when I was a baby, I threw up all over my aunt's shoulder after I had been fed a bowl of canned pears. But my uncle had just finished swinging me around his head. So who can blame me?" He pulls my supper toward him and finishes it off in one big gulp. "Until the day she died, Aunt Daisy claimed I was allergic to pears. But I haven't thrown up after eating them since."

"Maybe one day I will eat something and be allergic and die," I tell him. "In school, Mr. Howarth keeps Devin's EpiPen in his desk. Devin used to take care of it himself, but he kept losing it. Should we get an EpiPen for me? Just in case?"

Dad takes the dishes to the counter and dumps them in a messy heap. He bends down to open the door of the dishwasher. Then he closes it again when he sees that it is full. He pushes the dishes in the sink with a clatter.

"If the stuff in the dishwasher is clean, you have to put it away," I say. "If it's dirty, you have to turn it on." I get up from the table and open it again. "See? All clean."

"Okay. I'll unload. You put them away." Dad boosts me onto the counter.

I reach down for him to hand me the plates. "Do you think I might be allergic and we just don't know?"

"Tansy. There is absolutely no point in worrying about things that don't need worrying about. It may be better to be safe than sorry about lots of things. But right now we have more things to worry about than allergies."

But I can't help it. As I put things on the shelves in their proper places, I make a list in my head of all the things at Miss Stella's that might make me sick.

Artichoke hearts. They don't look like hearts at all.

Pita bread out of a package. Parveen's *Bebe-ji* makes theirs from scratch. She calls them *rotis*. The ones in Miss Stella's fridge look very old.

Omega-3 eggs. Do they have three yolks? Mom always says that double yolks are lucky. What would she say about three?

Bird's custard powder. Miss Stella used to have this for dessert when she was a kid, and she said she still likes it. She'll make it for me one day.

Toasted soy beans. She said they are good on salads. They look like nuts to me.

The dishwasher is empty, and I've put everything away before I can think of any more items for my list. Dad swings me down, and I go in the living room to do my homework.

When the phone rings, I am working on my last three math questions. Dad answers it in his bedroom. He must be listening most of the time, because I don't hear his voice very often.

"Was that Grandpa?" I ask him when he comes back. "Did you talk to Mom? I wanted to talk to her."

He sits on the couch next to me and pulls me against him. "Mom is on new medication that makes her very sleepy. We can talk to her in a couple of days. Okay?" He rubs his chin in my hair and gently pushes me away.

Maybe what Dad needs is a Trusted Other. His friend Paul has gone away for two years to the Arctic. Is that north or south? I used to know. And Dale and Jenny were really Mom's friends, and they haven't called lately.

I do not believe that Dad tells me everything. But I guess it's okay; I don't tell him everything either. Maybe I should ask Mr. Howarth if parents can talk to the school counselor.

CHAPTER 9

Super-Concentrated Miss Stella

Each day I get more used to going to Miss Stella's after school. But I still punch the button to our intercom on my way into the building every day. Just in case.

Mom never answers.

Dad and I came up with a special system. If I see a yellow stickie on our front door when I get home, I have to go on to Miss Stella's. If there is no stickie, I know Dad is at home and I go right in. But he still does not meet me at the door like Mom would.

I have only talked to Mom twice on the phone. Once she cried. The other time she sounded very far away. I told her about exploring Miss Stella's apartment and learning calligraphy so I can get a star for handwriting at school. I told her that I went to Parveen's house and ate Indian supper like the grown-ups while all the kids had pizza, and that we played with her auntie's wedding bracelets. All forty of them!

I told her that I miss peanut butter and jelly sandwiches for after-school snack, but that Miss Stella gives me other interesting stuff instead. But I told her not to worry. I do not have allergies. I will not fall over and get all blotchy in the face and not be able to breathe, like Devin did when he had another attack last week. Mr. Howarth saved his life again.

I even told Mom that Mr. Howarth will never be as nice as Ms. Peters from grade four. But I like him better now that he's saved Devin's life twice. I know he will save mine if I ever need saving.

I think she was listening to what I told her. But she didn't say much at all.

∾❧∾

One day when I knock on Miss Stella's door, she swings it open wide and says, "Ta-Dah!"

She is wearing a long silky black robe over her shorts and T-shirt. When she turns around I see a beautiful fire-breathing dragon in bright yellows and oranges on the back.

"What do you think?" she asks. Her wrinkly legs and arms are hidden in her robe. Her face is full of smiles, as if all her wrinkles were washed away.

"I love it," I say. "Are you going somewhere nice?"

"No such luck. This is pure ornament." She opens her arms wide again and turns around slowly. "I ordered this silk kimono from Japan months ago. At my age, there's not much to long for. But I have always wanted one, and it finally came today."

Today is the day I get to explore her bedroom. I feel funny on my exploring trips. But I sure like them! I did the living room and the kitchen and the dining room and the bathroom. Which means I have been coming here for four weeks.

Each time I'm done, I practice calligraphy on a list of my favorite things:

Kitchen

Cheese grater. When you wind it round and round, the cheese squirms out the middle.

A loopy thing for hanging bananas on to get ripe. Miss Stella hangs her shopping list from it with a bulldog clip.

Bulldog clips. There are lots in the drawer and you can use them for:

1. Hanging shopping lists from the banana ripener thing
2. Closing a bag of chips so they stay crisp for next time (We use them at home now, instead of elastic bands)
3. Clipping wet calligraphy to the curtain rail to dry
4. Taking the huge ones to school to threaten Devin and Ryan with (until Mr. Howarth confiscates them)
5. Giving one away to Parveen, who wanted one but didn't know what to do with it

Dining room

Calligraphy pens. They all have different nibs. Miss Stella says they are quite cheap, so when one fell out the window and Mr. 104 ran over it in his car, she said I was not to worry.

Two wine glasses with colored flowers all over them. We use them for juice sometimes. I believe it tastes better that way.

Living room

A pottery frog with a purple vest that used to hold Miss Stella's grandpa's tobacco. Now it just has a safety pin, an old movie ticket and some elastic bands. Sometimes wine gums when she wants to save some for herself. But there haven't been any in there for ages, so she must have found another hiding place. I am addicted to wine gums now.

The purple afghan Miss Stella covers me with if I have to stay late. She says I could use her room, but I like to fall asleep listening to the *scratch scratch* of her calligraphy. Right now she is hand-lettering a poetry book. She says the poems may not be literature, but they are special to the family of the person who wrote them, so they are just as important. It has taken her four months so far, and she has not even started the flourishes.

Bathroom

A leather pouch of jacks. Miss Stella bought them at a garage sale and showed me how to play. The bathroom is the best place as there is no carpet there and the ball bounces higher. She is better than me. But she says she started playing more than sixty years ago. Back then, she played "five stones" with little rocks, which was the same game.

A little brush for making your eyebrows straight. Mom had one, but I used it to paint with once and she never bought a new one.

That's all so far.

Miss Stella sways around in her new kimono to a Bee Gees tape while I have my snack. (No CD player at her house!) I know that "Staying Alive" is her favorite song because she plays it over and over again. I guess when you are as old as her, staying alive is the most important thing of all.

Dad despises the Bee Gees.

I worry that the candied pecans we made for salads might make me allergic, but my tongue is okay so far. So I put some on my plate. Oranges and pretzels are fine too.

I don't talk while I have my snack, because I know Miss Stella never answers when she is busy doing something else.

I lick the little salty chunks off the shiny brown pretzels while I take the calligraphy pens out of their roll and line them up in squares like tic-tac-toe. When I have eaten the oranges clean, I turn their nubby skins inside out and smile back at the white grinning shapes they make on my plate.

I pretend the pens are drumsticks and tap against the table while I wait for the Bee Gees to stop singing.

"Miss Stella?"

She stands still and folds her arms together so her hands disappear inside her sleeves. "Yes?"

"You should try to do two things at once sometimes," I tell her.

"Why?"

"I think it would be more efficient."

Miss Stella gives a little snort.

"I dance at home sometimes. But I can talk to Mom or Dad at the same time," I say.

"Tell me something, my little chickadee," she says in a funny voice.

"What?"

"Tell me three things you noticed about your snack. Or what it feels like to be wrapped up tight like a little mummy at night. Or the smell of the lobby as you come into the building. Or the taste of a wine gum. Can you?"

I fiddle with the pens while I think for a bit. But I can't come up with an answer. We've been out of wine gums for days!

"I like to be mindful when I'm doing things," Miss Stella says. "It's like super concentration. Thinking about just one thing at a time. So everything is fresh and memorable each time. Call me Super-Concentrated Miss Stella!"

"Like frozen orange juice!"

"You *are* super-concentrated sometimes, you know," she says. "But maybe you haven't noticed. Like your snacks and your funny bedtime ritual. It is important to be mindful as often as you can."

"Why?"

"Because it helps you be where you are and feel what you feel, without always rushing on to the next thing. And it helps you not worry about things."

When Miss Stella hugs me, I concentrate hard on her lovely silky kimono. It feels like I'm floating in a warm bath.

I stack my glass on my plate and line the pens back up in a row. How can I be super-concentrated with so many important things to think about? When will Mom get well? Are allergies catching? Will Dad get depressed like Mom? What will happen in the school holidays if Mom is still at Grandpa's and I have to stay here?

"Let me show you something." Miss Stella goes to the dresser where my calligraphy pages are stacked. As she flips through them, her sleeves flap like flags.

She picks up one sheet of writing and holds it in front of me. "In this one, you were just beginning and were hardly concentrating at all. I guess you thought it would be easy." Then she picks up another. "As you wrote these words, you were telling me about having supper at Parveen's house. And here…" She pulls out another one. "You were trying to decide whether you wanted to make chocolate chip cookies or cheese straws for your father.

"But this one…" She holds a sheet of the special white paper in front of me. It just has one word on it. *Tansy* in beautiful letters with hardly a glitch. "You did not say a word the entire time you worked on this," says Miss Stella. "You did not speak. Or look at me. I could have gone to China and you would not have missed me. See what you can create when you are super-concentrated?"

CHAPTER 10

Taking Care of Business

When I show Dad, he props the white paper with my name in beautiful calligraphy on the bookshelf. Then he stands back and looks at it a long time. He picks it up again and looks at it some more. "You did this?"

"Miss Stella is teaching me calligraphy."

"This is lovely work, Tan. Perhaps you'd like to send it to Mom."

"I can take it when we go see her. You said we could go when she was settled in at Grandpa's. Four weeks is a long time to get settled."

He sets the paper back on the shelf and sits in his favorite chair, pulling me down with him. When I am comfortable on his lap, I think that maybe this was why Mom went to stay with Grandpa instead of staying home where I can take care of her. Maybe being home with Grandpa makes Mom feel as warm and safe as I feel in Dad's arms.

When you feel depressed, I bet it is important to feel safe and warm.

Dad rubs his chin into my head. "Tansy, I have to tell you something."

"What?"

"You have to listen. Think carefully about what I'm going to tell you before you get mad."

I try to pull away to look at him, but he holds me close. "Tell me first. I can't make any promises," I say.

Dad takes a deep breath that I feel all down my back. "I told you that Mom was staying with Grandpa until she felt better," he says. "But that was not quite true."

"You lied?"

"Perhaps not quite a lie. But I let you believe something by not telling you the whole truth. Mom is very sick. Depression is like other diseases. To get better you have to have the right treatment."

"I thought that all she needed was to sit and look at the water and be taken care of by Grandpa.

While we take care of business here. And then she would be better and she could come home."

"It will take a bit more than that." Dad rubs my shoulder round and round. "We found a special doctor for Mom's depression. He takes just a few patients for six weeks at a time on a special program. That is where Mom is. At Dr. Graham's clinic."

"Mom is in the nuthouse?"

"Tansy!"

I haul myself off his lap and stare at him. "Devin and Ryan are right! My mom *is* a nutcase and she *is* at the funny farm!" I'm yelling and crying, and I don't care if the neighbors hear me. "You should have told me. I told everyone she was staying with Grandpa. You made me lie! You said we could go visit her. But she is a *nutcase*! And you never told me! I bet she will never come home now. When were you going to tell me *that*?"

I dash into my room and slam the door behind me.

In movies, people throw themselves on their beds and start crying loudly when everything's gone wrong or someone dies suddenly. I thought that was just make-believe.

But that is just what you do in real life when you find out that your worst enemies are right and that your dad has not been telling the truth. That is what you do when you want things to be like they used to be. Even if you can't remember what that was like. Because your mother has been depressed for so long.

And now she is in the nuthouse. Just like all the other loony tunes.

And she may never come home.

I must have fallen asleep. When I wake up, the room is dim and my face feels fat and hot. My nose is so plugged I think I may suffocate. So I start crying again.

"Tansy? May I come in?"

"Go away!"

"I will go away for a little while if you want me to. But I *will* come back." Dad's voice is very low and sad.

"Fine then!"

"Are you hungry?"

"No!"

I turn over and listen to his footsteps going down the hall.

I lied. I am hungry. So hungry that it feels like my stomach is meeting in the middle and not liking what it finds.

Have I had supper yet? Maybe it is breakfast time. I try to remember what homework I should have done and if I have done it yet.

I don't even know if it is yesterday or today, or what I have to do for school.

I would know if I was super-concentrated like Miss Stella.

So I decide to lie still and concentrate for a minute before I go to find something to eat.

CHAPTER 11

Those Scary Places Inside

Just yesterday—or maybe it was today—after Miss Stella explained about being mindful and super-concentrated, we went outside so I could practice by concentrating on the smell of summer coming.

I thought it was a silly idea. But it turned out to be kind of fun.

We sat in our chairs and closed our eyes.

Miss Stella told me to let go of all my other thoughts and just be part of the world around me. That took a while. Trying not to think about stuff makes you think about it harder.

"It's just like everything," she told me. "It will take practice. But you can start now. What can you smell?"

I wiggled in my seat until I was comfortable. Then I squeezed my eyes so no light came through. "Maybe a barbecue?"

"What else?"

"Can I change my mind? Not a barbecue. A hot dog being barbecued! I know that smell and I can't stand it."

"Don't bother about whether a smell is good or bad," she said. "A smell is a smell is a smell. What else?"

"Your cucumber soap from the bathroom. And the new roof next door. And car fumes. There is too much traffic around here."

"Mmm."

"And the tomato plants! I never knew they smelled when they are still growing."

After the smelling moment, we did a listening one. Then a touching one and a seeing one and a tasting one.

This is the list I wrote in my best calligraphy later. Miss Stella told me that when you are being super-concentrated about writing one thing, you should not be thinking about something else. Like what you might have for supper. Or if Dad will be home late. Or what the other person is noticing.

So while I wrote my list, I just concentrated on writing.

Taste

Hot dogs. I never knew you could taste what you can smell without tasting. If you know what I mean.

Touch

The hard edge of the chair under my legs.

Sun on my knees.

Something creepy-crawly running up my arm. I was going to shake it off, but Miss Stella said if I waited it out and just kept feeling it tickle as it crawled on me, it would stop eventually. And she was right.

Sound

Sirens. There are always lots of sirens around here.

Crinkly sounds from the breeze in the trees.

Mr. 101 driving his car into the parking lot. Then his door slamming.

A ball hitting a baseball bat in the park up the street.

Seeing

A crow walking all over the carport roof like he owns the place. Crows are the bossiest birds. But I shouldn't have said that. Miss Stella said being super-concentrated is not about judging. But that can be hard.

The branch of the tree tipping over as an invisible squirrel scampers along it.

My toes curling over the white railing.

Miss Stella sitting in her chair next to me with her hands folded on her lap and her eyes closed.

Her wrinkles. I saw all of them. Every one. And I noticed they are not ugly at all. They are just wrinkles.

Now as I lie in bed, I try to stop thinking about what happened yesterday and just concentrate on today instead. But it's hard!

I roll over and over until I'm all mummified like the middle of a sausage roll, with just one toe sticking out from under the covers.

Then I tug my arms out and reach under my bed for a scrap of paper and a pencil. And I write a new list:

A little breeze trickling through the window.

My chest all tight like someone has their hands around it and is squeezing it.

My ears stretching to hear what Dad is doing.

The silence Dad makes in the other room.

The lumpy shadowy look of the clothes on the chair. I should have put them away. But forget that last part. It was judging. They were just clothes on a chair.

A little twitch in my left foot.

A huge hole inside me that won't be filled up until Mom comes home.

Trembly feelings all up and down me that I think is worry about Mom and all the bad things that could happen at home and at school that she needs to be here for.

A little quiet place inside all the holes and trembles. Maybe this is the place that knows Dad will take care of what he can take care of. And we can worry about the rest later.

When I am done, part of me wants to get up and find Dad so I can tell him I am sorry I made a fuss before. Even though everything I said is still true and it hurts so much it is just like being pricked all over by hundreds of pins.

But instead I lie still and practice not worrying about later or what comes next. Just being there.

Miss Stella said that sometimes just being there is the best place to be.

CHAPTER 12

Guaranteed Allergy-Proof

I am about to drift off to sleep again when a little knock comes on the door. Then it opens and a glint of light sneaks through.

"Tansy?" says Dad.

"Mmm?"

"Feeling better?"

"A bit." I sit up and lean back on my pillow.

Dad has a halo around him from the hallway light. "Can I come in now?"

"Okay."

He sits on my bed. He hands me a plate as he switches on the bedside lamp.

"What kind of cookies are these?" I ask.

"I finally got them at the health food store. They are guaranteed allergy-proof. *Manufactured in a nut-free facility.* It says so on the package."

I bite into one. "I can take these to school for a snack." I say with my mouth full.

"Are you ready to talk?" asks Dad. "I think we need to."

"Okay." That scary place inside me twitches, but I close my eyes and let it be. I take another bite of the nut-free cookie. "Can you start? I don't know how."

"Sure." Dad clears his throat.

Suddenly I get it. He is scared too! But he is grown up, so he is not allowed to act out and be rude to friends and pick fights and sulk and throw himself on the bed in tears like they do in the movies.

I bet the scared place inside Dad is even bigger than mine. As well as worrying that Mom might not get better, he has to take care of me. "Go on, Dad." I hand him a cookie and watch him nibble it while he thinks.

"I should have told you about Mom and the treatment program right at the beginning. I apologize."

"I forgive you." I pull my duvet up to my chest and wrap my arms around myself tight.

"We have to think of it as taking care of Mom the best way we can. It does not matter—not a bit—what your friends think about your mom being sick. Or where she needs to go to get better." He taps gently on my bundle of bedcovers. "It matters what *you* think. But I am sorry that your friends make you feel bad about it."

"They are not *my* friends."

"You said Ryan was one of the ones making fun. You went to preschool with him. Remember? You went to the same parties. Perhaps you are not friends now, but he's been part of your life for quite a few years."

"He is friends with Devin now."

"Ah, well. Poor Devin. Think what *he* has to deal with, with his allergies and all. Maybe he is mean to you because making you angry is easier than thinking about how scared he is."

"Of what?"

Dad takes the plate off the bed and puts it on my bedside cupboard. "Think about it a little, Tansy. I know you can figure it out. Now. We need to get something straight here."

"Okay."

"Your mother *will* come home. I don't know when. Not yet. She only has ten days left of the program and is doing well. They have given her different drugs that are helping. When the six weeks is up, she will spend a couple more weeks resting up at Grandpa's. You know how close they are. We will visit her, and perhaps you can even stay for a few days and help Grandpa out. Then when she goes back to the clinic…" he puts one hand on my shoulder, as if he knows what I am going to say, "…it will just be for one day. They will assess her and maybe adjust the medications. And then she will come home. We hope."

Dad takes a great long trembly breath and looks away from me. I can see tears shining at the edge of his eyes.

"I'm sorry I yelled, Dad."

He looks at me again, and the tears are gone. Men must have fewer tears in them than women. "You have nothing to be sorry about, Tan." He stands and picks up my plate. "Do you want to get up for a while? Come into the living room? We can play a game of Sorry. It must be my turn to win. We'll make smoothies—

a couple of bananas are about to go bad and we should use them." He sees me scrunch up my face. "Oh. Right. You despise bananas now. Well, we can use ice cream and chocolate powder. Okay?"

When I get up, Dad hugs me hard. I hug him back, feeling his shirt, smelling his smell, feeling safe for now.

CHAPTER 13

Googling Miss Stella

I tuck my list inside Harry Potter and brush my hair. Then I go to find Dad.

He is sitting at the computer in his bedroom.

"What are you doing?" I ask.

"There was something I wanted to show you."

I stand behind him and peer at the screen. "What?"

"I googled your Miss Stella. Guess what I found?"

"Miss Stella's in Google?"

"All over it, like a dirty shirt."

This is a dumb expression. But I know it means all over the place, not a judgment about laundry.

"*Stella Vickers was trained at the Slade School in London and within ten years had earned an international reputation for her work on illuminated texts, found in important collections worldwide,*" reads Dad. "More than seven thousand web pages mention her, one way or another."

"What is an illuminated text?"

"A book that is very carefully hand-produced, with special lettering and ornamentation."

"I guess ornamentation is all the pictures and patterns that go with the words. She taught me how to do some. Flourishes, she calls them. Why is she famous?"

"Her work is considered the best in the world. It has been in exhibitions. The Queen even has one of her books."

"Our queen?"

"So it says here." Dad clicks at the computer some more. "Your Miss Stella is quite the dark horse. Not letting on how good she is, or how well-known."

"But she is poor! Miss Stella has no car. Or a computer or a cell phone! How can she be famous?"

Dad grins at me. "Being renowned for something does not make you rich, necessarily. And not having a car or a cell phone does not mean you are poor. You know that Mom and I taught you not to judge by appearances."

"And not to judge a book by its cover!"

"That too. Next time you see her, you can ask Miss Stella all about life as a famous calligrapher. Looks like you may be on your way to being one too." Dad looks across the room to my *Tansy* sign on his dresser.

He turns off the computer. "Come on. You find the Sorry board while I make those smoothies. We'll have one of those new cookies too."

After school the next day, Parveen gets to come home with me for a while. At last! I think it's because she told her grandma I know someone who knows the Queen. Her *Bebe-ji* has pictures of the royal family all over their house. Specially Princess Diana, who is pretty, but dead now.

Miss Stella is in the lobby when we get there. She is holding a box. "Here you are, then. Your dad was called in to work so you're stuck with me. Do you reckon we can find something to keep us busy? And who is this?"

I introduce Parveen, and Miss Stella shakes hands with her. Upstairs, it feels funny having Parveen in the apartment that is not mine but feels like it is. She looks around at all the stuff I am so used to seeing.

"What's in the box?" I ask Miss Stella.

She puts it on the table. "Come and look. Brushes galore. All the way from China."

She lets Parveen and me open the box. Inside are layers and layers of lovely papers in all colors, so thin you can almost see through them. One layer of paper, then a layer of brushes with bamboo handles. Long yellow handles with dark bristles. Then more paper and more brushes, until we get to the bottom.

"Fifty brushes. Think they will last me?" says Miss Stella.

"Chinese brush work is very difficult," I tell Parveen. "Miss Stella says I can try soon if I keep doing as well as I am with my calligraphy."

She looks impressed.

We spread all the brushes out on the table and run our fingers along the bristles.

Parveen smiles as she strokes her pretty fingers along the brushes as if they were piano keys. She has a lovely smile with very white teeth. I bet she flosses more than me.

"Find a snack, you two," says Miss Stella. "Then we can figure out how to spend our afternoon."

I am just pulling the box of triangle cheese out of the fridge when Miss Stella reaches in beside me. "I found this for you." She hands me a jar. "You might want to use it for your school lunches."

Parveen reads the label. "Pea butter? We have *dahl,* which is made of peas. *Bebe-ji* makes it as smooth as butter. Maybe this is the same."

"Similar, perhaps," Miss Stella replies. "It says it is ideal for nut-free diets."

I remember the *manufactured-in-a-nut-free-facility* cookies Dad bought. If Devin wasn't allergic, we would not have to worry about stuff that could kill him by accident.

I have a thought. "Hey, Parveen. If I take Devin a sandwich made specially with nut-free bread and pea butter, do you think he might stop giving me a hard time?"

She shrugs.

Then I shrug.

"How about you tell me about this hard time Devin gives you," says Miss Stella.

I have never bothered her with stuff about Devin and Ryan and their mean jokes about nutcases and funny farms. When Mr. Howarth asked me if I have a Trusted Other who I can talk to, I said Dad. But sometimes Dad is not enough. And anyway, I did not want to tell him what Devin had been teasing me about.

I have a pulling feeling inside where my heart hurts. I close my eyes and put my hands on my chest. I feel the hard bone under my shirt and wait for the ache to pass. But it is still there.

When I open my eyes, Parveen is sitting at the table with a handful of brushes, running her fingers gently across the soft bristles. "Go on. Tell," she says.

Then instead of waiting for me, she does the telling. "Those mean kids? There are two of them. And sometimes their other friends. They yell at Tansy and tell lies to everyone else about her mom. May I have a snack, please? And a glass of water?"

In the kitchen I put five cheese triangles, a handful of almonds and a bunch of dried apricots on a plate. When I eat them, I hardly ever think of Miss Stella's wrinkly skin anymore.

I fill two glasses with water and watch the patterns it makes as it pours.

By the time Miss Stella has cleared the table, I know I will tell her about Devin and Ryan and all the rotten things they say about me and my mother. Things that are true. But not right.

For just a minute I remember that I had planned to ask her about being famous and the Queen's book. But that will come later, I think.

Right now I know I need a Trusted Other.

So I look at Miss Stella sitting waiting across the table, and I take a deep breath.

CHAPTER 14

Poor Devin, Poor Me

Parveen and I have both eaten our snack by the time we finish telling Miss Stella all about Devin and Ryan sneaking up on me to make fun of my mom, and telling me that if Devin dies of a nut allergy it will be my fault. And yelling at me in the playground and riding around and around us on their bikes on the way home from school.

Miss Stella has not eaten a thing. But I know her by now. She will not eat and do anything else at the same time. When she eats or reads or smells the tomatoes grow or watches the ivy climb up the trellis or walks to the store, Miss Stella does one thing at a time and leaves everything else until later.

I asked her the other day if she is Super-Concentrated Miss Stella even when she goes to the bathroom. She just laughed.

"You are so brave to put up with all that," says Miss Stella when we are done telling. "Have you told your teacher?"

"Mr. Howarth knows," I say. "Maybe. I think he heard Devin once."

"Then why does he not speak to the boy?"

I shrug.

"Has he been a teacher very long?" Miss Stella asks.

"Remember on the first assembly, the principal said this was his first job?" says Parveen. I watch her twirl the end of her braid in her fingers. It looks like it would make a good calligraphy brush!

"And we were lucky to have him?" she continues. "He went to our school when he was a kid."

"I see," says Miss Stella. As if she really does.

"What do you see?" I ask.

"Poor man must be pretty scared. His first job and a bully in the class."

"Devin is not a bully. Not really."

"Of course he is. Even if what he says is true."

"But it's *not* true," says Parveen. "Tansy's mom is not in a nuthouse. That's a mental hospital. This time she's just away at Tansy's grandpa's."

"My mom is in a clinic," I tell her. "It's like a mental hospital. My mom is really sick. Depression is more than just being sad."

"Oh." Parveen runs her finger down one of the ripples of her braid without looking at me.

I suddenly remember something. "You said Mr. Howarth was scared, which is why he has not said anything to Devin. What did you mean?" I ask Miss Stella.

"Bullying is something teachers need to learn to deal with. It's part of his job, you could say. But even if he is really well-trained, that is a great responsibility. Just like dealing with thirty children every day."

"We only have twenty-seven kids in our class." Parveen flips her hair back over her shoulder.

"Devin is scared too," says Miss Stella. "Which is why he is a bully."

I remember Dad saying something like that to me too. But why would Devin be scared? I have never figured out the answer.

Then a thought comes into my head. *Because he could die at any minute.*

Suddenly it is like someone has dumped a bucket of cold water over me. My skin feels as if it is shrinking. How would I feel if a tiny trace of nuts got on my skin or in my mouth and I fell over and my tongue got thick and there was no more air to breathe?

I would be scared all the time.

"Poor Devin." I think I am saying it to myself, but the words get out.

"Devin was mean to you," says Parveen. "Names are bad. I wish your mom was not in a clinic. You could have told me. But yelling at people in your class is bad. Why are you sorry for *him*?"

"Because he thinks he could die."

A huge tide of tears keeps coming. I swallow hard to keep them away. But it doesn't work. I am such a baby.

Miss Stella gets up and puts her arms around me. I feel little rocking movements and smell her cucumber soap and feel her scratchy hair against my cheek.

Poor Devin, I think.

I cry and cry.

Parveen rips the silver paper off one little cheese triangle, then another, while Miss Stella rocks me and rocks me.

I use a whole bunch of tissues. They sit in a wet clump on the table. Parveen is trying out an easy calligraphy pen and is pretty good at it. I can read her name upside down across the table. I watch her write it again and again.

In a little while, when I'm still trying to catch my gulpy breath, Miss Stella goes outside to deadhead her flowers. That means she takes off all the dead flowers and crumbles them up and puts them back in her pots, where she says Mother Nature takes care of them.

When I think about how my mother is not around to take care of *me*, I cry some more. *Poor me.*

Miss Stella rubs my back as she passes me on her way into the kitchen.

At last, when I stop crying and can breathe again, I sniff rather loudly. "Tomorrow I will take a pea butter sandwich to Devin," I say. "It will be a peace offering."

Parveen turns her paper over. I should tell her to wait until the other side is dry.

But instead I take a piece of good paper from Miss Stella's special drawer. I pick up my favorite pen, which we keep in a red satin box. "I have a plan," I say. And I dip my pen in the ink and very carefully start a new list using my best calligraphy.

CHAPTER 15

Taking the Bull by the Horns

"You make me very proud," Dad says after I tell him about my list. It took me a long time, and I concentrated so hard that I hardly noticed when he came to pick me up.

We are eating fish and chips out of paper. If Mom were here she would heat plates while Dad goes to the fish-and-chip shop. She would set out cutlery and placemats and napkins.

Dad puts the open package in the middle of the table. We eat with our fingers; we will wash our hands later.

I have put the list on the bookshelf, out of the way of greasy fingers, while Dad and I have our supper. I know what it says by heart. It took me almost an hour to write. Miss Stella walked Parveen home while I finished it. So even she does not know what it says.

While we eat, I tell Dad what I have decided to do. Which means I hardly concentrate at all as I peel off the batter and eat it separately and take one bite of fish, then one of chips. It's the way I always eat it.

My list says:

1. *Give Devin the pea butter sandwich and tell him that I am sorry he is allergic.*
2. *Tell Mr. Howarth about the bullying so he can take care of it. He is the grown-up.*
3. *Tell Mr. H that I really appreciate the advice about having a Trusted Other, but I have Dad and Miss Stella and Parveen, so I won't need to see Ms. Carlton, the school counselor.*
4. *Offer to show and tell the class about my calligraphy and tell them all about famous Miss Stella.*
5. *Write a letter to Mom in my best calligraphy so she knows how much I miss her.*

"I must be full, because I feel sick," says Dad when there's still a bunch of cold chips left. This is an old joke, and we laugh each time we say it. I said it once when I was little, and no one will let me forget it.

"You came up with this yourself?" Dad asks when I have finished telling him what I plan to do. He rolls the paper around the chips and takes them into the kitchen. I hear the garbage can open and then close. I should tell him that Mom would put it all in a plastic bag first. The kitchen will smell now, even after he takes out the garbage. But Dad has to figure this stuff out for himself. Just like I have to.

"It was all my idea. But it will be hard to do," I say. Already I am nervous.

"How badly do you want Devin to feel better about his allergies. Even just a little?"

"Quite a bit."

"And how much do you want your teacher to take care of you while you're in school?"

"A lot."

"I think writing a letter to Mom is a fine idea. It will help you get things off your chest." He brings me a big glass of OJ and sets it on the table. "Drink up. You need your vitamins," he says. "Sometimes the only thing to do is take the bull by the horns."

I drink my juice in three gulps. "Bulls have very sharp horns."

"Aren't you the joker!" Dad says. "I am very proud of you, Tansy." His voice is all choky. "Your mother would be too. And this weekend might be a very good time to give her your letter. So you had better get on it."

My glass tips over as I jump up. I throw myself at Dad so hard he nearly falls over too. "Are we going to see Mom? This weekend? Does that mean she is better now? Has she graduated from the clinic?"

"Yes. Yes. And yes." Dad picks me up in a bear hug and swings me around. I bend my knees because last time I knocked over Mom's favorite lamp. I bet I've grown since I saw her. How long ago was that? So many weeks I have lost count.

Dad puts me down and nuzzles my neck. "We will see how things go. She is not sure she is quite ready to come home. Let's get to Grandpa's and see how it goes. Okay?"

I feel so happy and light, I think I could fly. I am so excited about Mom being better. But one thing at a time, as Miss Stella says. "I want this to be the best letter ever," I tell Dad. "And in my best calligraphy." I pick up my list again. I read it slowly, to make sure that everything I need to do is there.

"Chores first. Calligraphy later," says Dad.

"There are no dishes, Dad. We ate supper on paper and you threw it all away."

We have to start changing our ways soon. Things will be different when Mom comes home.

CHAPTER 16

In Her Own Words

On Sunday morning we are just packing our stuff into Dad's backpack for our trip to see Mom when Miss Stella drops by.

"I have a little something for you." She is holding a square package with a bump on it. It is wrapped in one of the old maps she found at the thrift store. Miss Stella recycles and does not use regular wrapping paper.

"Can I open it? Stay while I open it."

"Not too long, though. I have a date for a walk around Stanley Park with a friend."

Sometimes I forget Miss Stella might have other friends. When I go to her house she never makes calls or has people over. We just spend our time with each other. I bet her other friends think they are the only ones she has too.

Dad cuts the string with his Swiss Army knife. Then I unwrap the paper very carefully so I can look at the map later.

Inside is the most beautiful book I have ever seen. I hardly dare touch it. The cover is all smudgy greens and red. "I have been working on this for a while," says Miss Stella. "But this seems like the right day to give it to you. That paper is handmade," she adds. "And that special binding on the spine is called Coptic." All down the spine are little rows of string and knots. "It was bound by my friend Linda in Nelson."

I stroke the book and turn it over and over. "Thank you. It is lovely."

"But there is more," says Miss Stella. "Look inside."

The first page is blank, so I know it is a notebook. I turn the next page.

Tansy's Book

In Her Own Words

For her eyes only

"My own calligraphy notebook! I love it." I give her a big hug, breathing in the smell of her cucumber soap.

"Not everyone gets their own handmade book with calligraphy by the famous Stella Vickers," Dad says.

"Oh, hush, Lew," says Miss Stella. "You missed something, Tansy."

When she rattles the paper, a long thin box slips out. Inside is a pen. "That's a special felt pen for calligraphy," she says. "No ink required, so you can take your notebook and your pen and write anywhere."

We are only going to the Sunshine Coast for the day. But as we get in the car, Miss Stella calls good-bye from her balcony as if we plan to be away for ages. "Have a wonderful visit. And enjoy the ferry trip." She has been watering her balcony, and it *drip-drip-drips* down the wall, like a clock ticking.

"Thank you for my book," I call back. From below, I can only see one of her arms flapping and a strand of her hair that has escaped from her messy bun. "Don't be late for your friend."

As we drive away, I open the notebook again and run my fingers over the title page. "Isn't this beautiful, Dad? But I am afraid to write in it. What if I mess it up?"

"It's your book. No one will see whether you mess up or not."

I flip through the book and find something I did not see before. On every single page, Miss Stella has made a little ink drawing of a tansy flower.

I think of all the time and concentration it has taken Miss Stella to make such a perfect gift.

And while I am thinking about this, I forget to worry about what will happen when we get to the Sunshine Coast and see Mom for the first time in weeks.

CHAPTER 17

The Best Girls in the World

When we drive up the gravel road to Grandpa's house, he is standing on the porch shaking a rug over the railing.

"There you are, then." He bends down at the top of the stairs and hauls me into a big hug. I can feel the tight muscles in his arms from all the woodcutting. His cheek is bristly and his mustache smells smoky.

"Where is Mom?"

"Down by the water. I suggest you go down to see her one at a time. She's a bit shaky."

"You go, Dad." I feel shy. Will Mom still be crying? Will she recognize me?

"We could go together. We can take it slowly," Dad says.

But Grandpa puts one hand on his arm. "You go ahead, Lew. Tansy and I will go inside and catch up on all our news."

"I need our bag."

When I get back from the car, I see Dad walking down the slope to the chairs where we always sit to count stars. "Come on, Tan. Let's put some coffee on," says Grandpa. He makes horrible coffee, Dad says. I can smell that he must have made some already today.

His house always looks like a campsite. He leaves blankets all over the place, stacks of books and greasy tools on tables, and clothes piled on any old chair. But today everything has been put away and cleaned up.

"You hungry? I have muffins and fruit. Homemade."

"Muffins?" Mom is a great baker.

"Fresh from the oven this morning. I'll take the bottoms if you want the tops." Grandpa and I always share them that way.

"Did Mom make these?"

He sets a stack of plates and cutlery at the table. "'Fraid not, lovey. Louella Harris. Remember her? She's taken it upon herself to help fatten up your mother. Fresh muffins to take every time I visit her at the clinic. A double batch when she heard you were on your way."

He stirs three spoonfuls of sugar into his coffee. Then one more. "Your mom is doing very well. This house is shipshape, thanks to her. Now, juice or milk?"

Dad takes forever. When I peek out of the window there is nothing to see. Just two chickadees dancing around the bird feeder. And down on the lake someone sitting in a boat.

Grandpa chatters on. He gets up and down from the table, and then he goes back and forth to the counter. He peeks out the window when he thinks I am not looking.

If she was here, Mom would tell him to *Sit still for heaven's sake.*

I show him my special book. I tell him how Dad and I will decorate my bike for sports day next week. Then I tell him about the calligraphy and the letter I have written Mom.

When Grandpa asks if he can see the letter, I tell him it is private. That I wrote it for Mom in my own words and for her eyes only.

"You are one brave girl. Naming you after such a sturdy and persistent wildflower was the perfect thing to do," says Grandpa. "I have the best girls in the world!" His face gets all pink when he is excited.

At last I hear Dad walking up the stairs. When he comes in the house, he goes straight to the coffeepot and pours a cup.

"Can I go now?" I ask.

Dad's face is blotchy and his eyelashes are wet. But he is smiling. "Sure. Mom is eager to see you."

I walk down the hill, trying not to run. Little waves glint on the lake. Leaves shiver in the trees. My stomach feels flickery, and my hands are sweaty. But I let the flickering and the sweatiness be. When I get to the bottom of the hill, I stand for a minute, looking at Mom's back as she stares at the water. "Mom?"

She turns around. Then she puts out her arms, and I walk right into them.

Mom is just the same. But different.

She reminds me of kids on the first day of school. Everyone has new clothes and fresh haircuts. Everyone is on their best behavior.

I have not seen Mom's dress before, or her shoes. Her hair looks like she had it cut. I wonder how long it will take her to go back to being her usual self, like kids on the second day of school.

Mom and I talk a bit. But not much. There are lots of silences between us.

She tells me about the birds she has been watching, sitting here by the water. About some of the other people at the clinic. One lady cleaner is always happy to sit and talk to Mom or anyone else who needs company. Maybe for now she's Mom's Trusted Other.

She says, "I will be home soon. Will you be pleased?" But she is looking out over the water. Not at me.

We sit side by side in the chairs. I look at the sun dancing on the glinty water.

I try to let the tight place in my chest be. I try to stop worrying about what I should say. For a while I don't even think about the letter I wrote that is still in the pocket of Dad's bag in Grandpa's house. I don't think about when will be the best time to give it to her or if she will smile when she reads it. Or if it will make her cry.

I try not to worry about what will happen next and just practice being here.

I see a fish make a little splash. I hear the breeze rustle the leaves and a loon far down the lake call to its mate and the clatter of a bucket along the shore.

When Mom moves her hand from her chair to mine, I put my fingers on hers and stroke and stroke and stroke.

CHAPTER 18

Show and Tell

Mr. Howarth said I could show and tell about callig-raphy in the last art class of the term. So I work on my presentation after school every day. I make sure each word is perfect. Like all those books that made Miss Stella famous. She showed me pictures of some of them. One of them took almost two years!

Mom came home last weekend for a visit. Dad said he needed to spend some time alone with her, so I had lots of time at Miss Stella's to write in my new book and learn some new flourishes and practice my report.

While Mom was here, it was not quite like normal. But it feels like it might be soon.

Maybe I knew this stuff already, but this is what I wrote in my new notebook about some of the things I noticed this weekend:

Dad puts his hand on the back of Mom's neck when they talk in the kitchen before dinner.

Mom flicks her fingers against her leg when it gets quiet for a minute.

When Dad talks about something that might happen soon, Mom just smiles and then looks somewhere else. Or changes the subject.

Although Mom was home, everything felt the same as when she was gone. I still miss her, even when she is at home.

There are dust bunnies under the couch that I see when I lie on the floor reading.

The lamp I broke when Dad swung me around still works, but the crack shows.

Mom did not notice either of these things.

I was happy to be at Miss Stella's.

Her wrinkles are beautiful.

The morning I am to give my report, I read it to Dad first.

"You were word perfect. You will be a hit," he says afterwards. Then he makes my breakfast. I have told him all about what Super-Concentrated Miss Stella told me about mindfulness. I think he understands now that doing two things at once is not always necessary.

My egg is perfect today. The toast is still in rectangles, but it does not really matter.

I am nervous when I pick up Parveen. "I will be rooting for you," she says.

Of course she will. She is a Trusted Other.

Art is first class of the day, and Mr. Howarth says that we will start with my report about calligraphy before we work on our collages. When everyone is settled, he steps aside so I can stand next to his desk.

Then I take a deep breath and begin.

All about my famous sitter and calligraphy
By Tansy Hill
While my mom is away at a clinic being treated for depression, I got a new sitter.

I stare very hard at my paper so I can't look at Devin and Ryan.

Her name is Miss Stella Vickers. And she is famous. She is a famous calligrapher. Even the Queen has one of her books.

I hear Erin Warren at the front whisper, "The Queen!" But I keep reading.

Calligraphy is like handwriting. But it is more special and lots harder to do.

Miss Stella said it was started hundreds of years ago in Turkey. And China.

Miss Stella is teaching me to do it too. You don't use a computer. You need to use a special pen like this.

I hand one to Mr. Howarth to pass around.

I have to be super-concentrated when I do it so it turns out just right.

Like this.

I take the white envelope from behind my report and hold it up high so everyone can see. It says in big letters *A letter to Mom—for her eyes only. From Tansy.*

Each word is perfect. Underneath are two different flourishes Miss Stella taught me.

This is a special letter for my mother who has been away for weeks and weeks.

I still have not given the letter to Mom yet. Dad says I will know when the time is right.

I tried to tell my mom everything that has been going on while she has been away. But not enough to worry her.

Calligraphy is hard to do, like lots of things. But if you are super-concentrated like me and Miss Stella, you will find it easier to do.

I pick up my book from Mr. Howarth's desk and hold it open so everyone can see the title page.

This is the book Miss Stella made me. It is very special. It is one of a kind.

It is my own calligraphy book.

Maybe when I am as famous as Miss Stella, I will teach the kids I babysit how to do calligraphy.

If you ask me later, I can show you too.

CHAPTER 19

One Letter at a Time

I am all out of breath when I finish. When I look up, Parveen claps so hard her braid swings. Then Mr. Howarth applauds too, and everyone in the class joins in.

Devin and Ryan look at each other. Since I gave Devin the pea butter sandwich and the cookie manufactured in a nut-free facility, he stays away from me. Like he is scared of me, maybe.

Perhaps Mr. Howarth gave Devin and Ryan a good talking to. I think Miss Stella was right that it is his job to stop the bullies. I feel better now I have told him about it.

These days I hardly ever think about being allergic because, as Dad says, I don't have time to worry about everything.

"That was an excellent report," Mr. Howarth says again at the end of the day. There's still gunky collage glue all over my fingers, and I'm trying to pick it off. "Thank you for telling us about your famous Miss Vickers," he says.

"I call her Miss Stella," I tell him. "But you're welcome."

Parveen is standing by the lockers, waiting to walk home with me.

"And I hope your mother gets better soon," says Mr. Howarth. He pats my arm and heads for the staff room.

I look at the papers in my hand. It took forever to write my report in perfect calligraphy. I am going to save it for Mom to read, when she is up to it. Until then, I will keep it safe with the letter in the back of my special calligraphy book.

Parveen and I walk home together as far as the corner. Now that *Bebe-ji* knows Miss Stella has not actually met the Queen, maybe Parveen will not be able to come to my house again.

I pull the key from around my neck and open the front door. My hand does not go to the intercom anymore unless I want it to.

A little yellow stickie flaps from my door, so I head down the hallway to Miss Stella's apartment.

Only three more days before Dad takes me to spend the summer at Grandpa's. I wonder what the summer will be like now that Mom is almost well.

What will it be like without Miss Stella?

I know she will be here waiting for me on her jungly balcony when I come back. Meanwhile, we can write the most beautiful letters to each other. Word by word. One letter at a time.

I will be super-concentrated as I write each one.

But right now, I knock on the door of apartment 405 and waggle my fingers over the peephole so Miss Stella knows it is me.

Lois Peterson wrote short stories and articles for adults for twenty years before turning to writing for kids. Recently retired from her job in a library, she lives in Surrey, British Columbia, where she writes, reads and teaches creative writing to adults, teens and children. Check out her website at www.loispeterson.net.